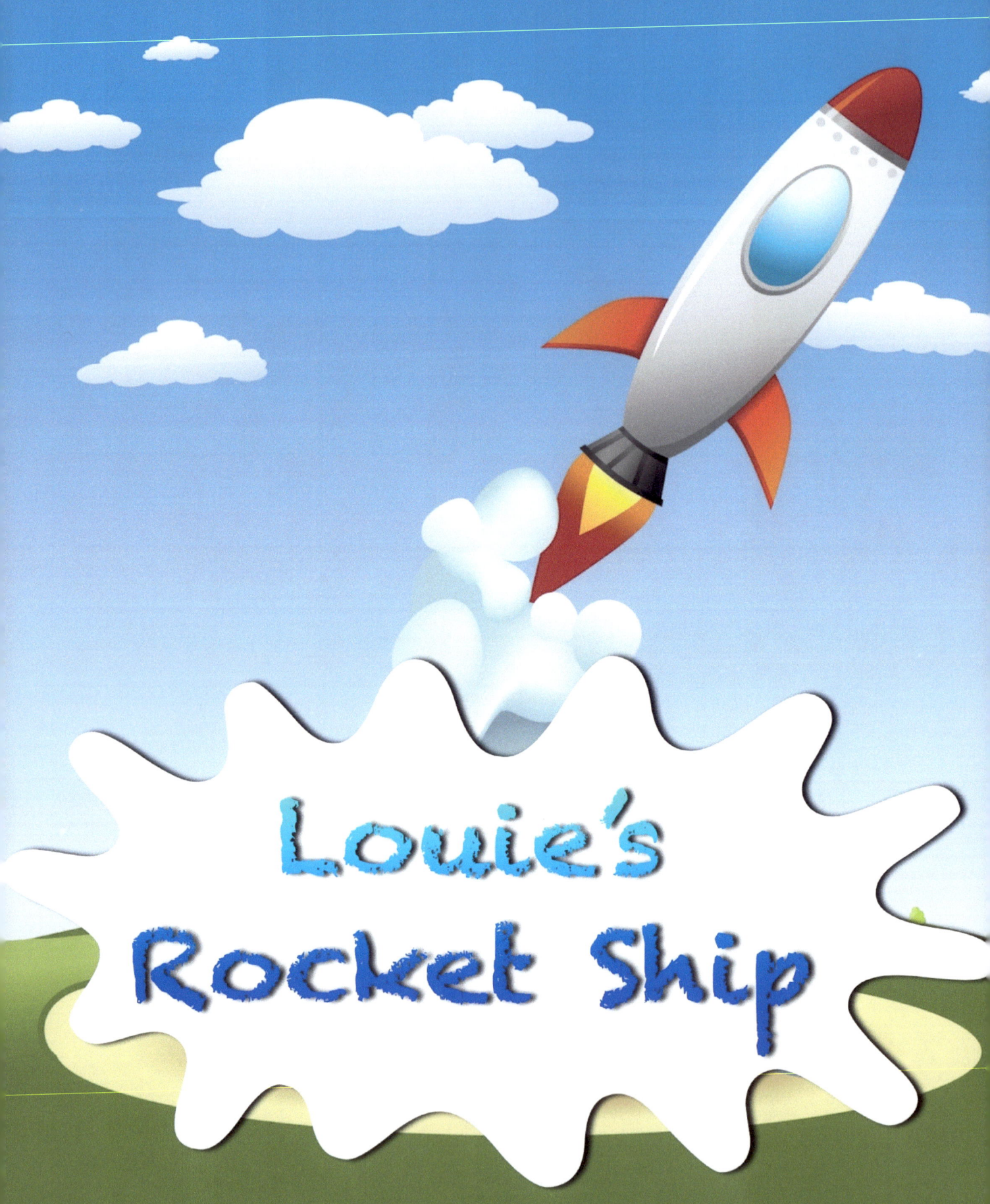

# Louie's Rocket Ship

**Written by**
Marion Jones
Samantha Smith

**Edited by**
P. J. Jones

Blue Bunny Agency
London

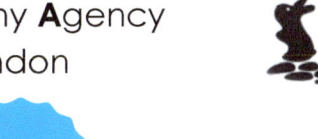

3

# Copyright

**Louie's Rocket Ship**

A series of books about Louie and Ethan's Dreamtime Adventure bedtime stories.

All rights reserved.
No part of this publication may be reproduced, distributed or transmitted in any form by any means, without prior written permission.

http://bit.ly/BlueBunnyAgency

Publishers Note:
This work is fiction.
Any association to names, places and incidents is the imagination of the Author.
Any resemblance to actual people, living or dead is completely coincidental.

ISBN: 978-0-9934180-5-1

This edition published March 2017
by The Blue Bunny Agency

www.Facebook.com/BlueBunnyAgency

Illustrations by Dreamstime .com

© The Blue Bunny Agency

Ethan tells Louie all about his school project. Rocket ships, the Space Station and the moon. Louie's imagination runs wild, which sets them on an adventure to build their own rocket ship.

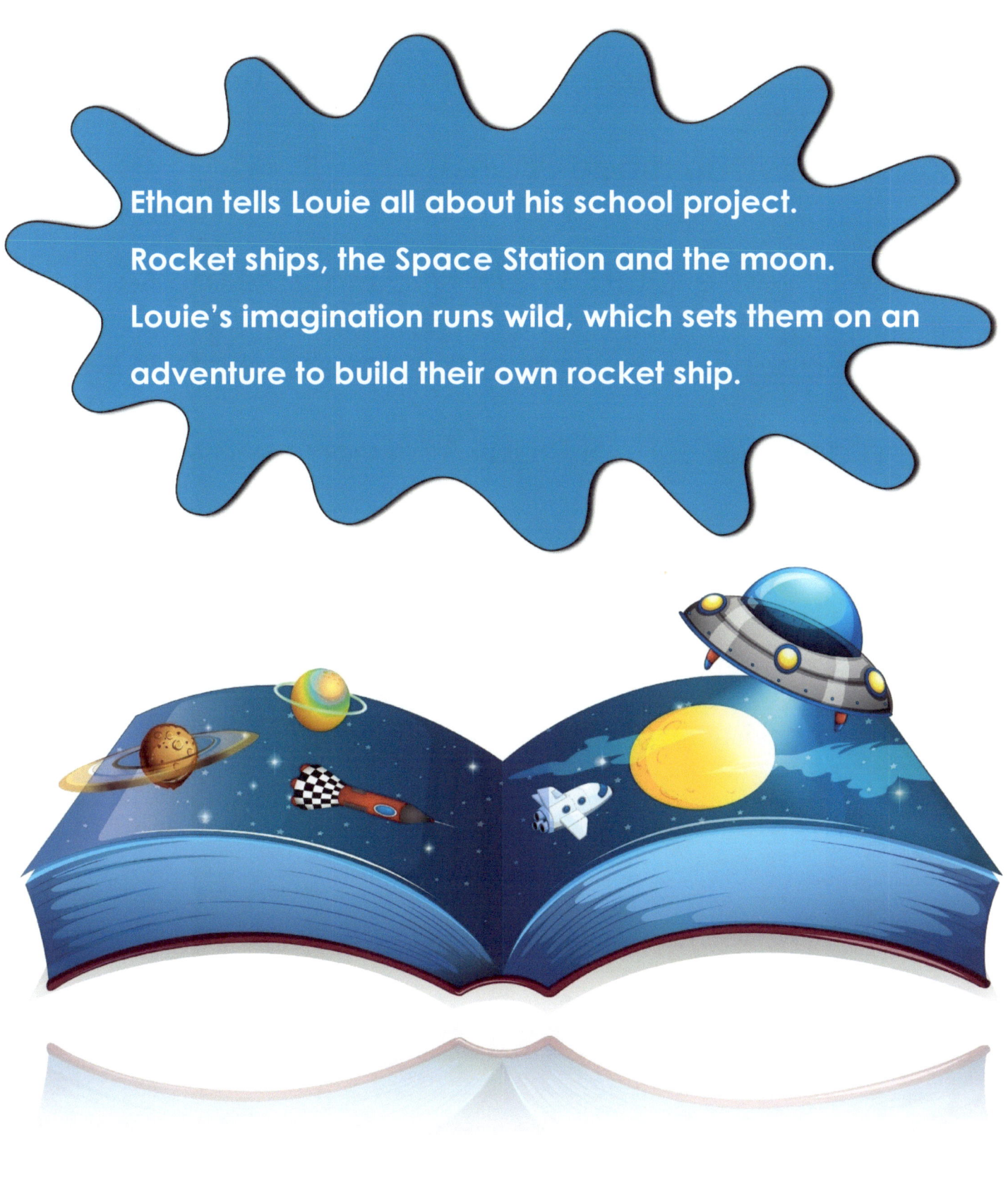

The school door flew open, Ethan ran out waving a model rocket, he made in class.

Louie was very excited, listening to Ethan telling Mum and him about his project. "Mum, guess what we were talking about at school today." "I don't know, Ethan, what did you learn today?" Mum replied.

"Our teacher showed how to build a rocket and talked about going into outer space," Ethan was smiling; he loved school.

On the way home Ethan told his brother all about what he had learned in class, rockets, space and the moon.

They walked home together talking about how to make a rocket.  As soon as they reached the house they ran upstairs, where

Ethan pulled out his school book, to show Louie.

They emptied their toy boxes and start building a rocket, when Mum reminded them that Gran had bought them a cardboard rocket.

With Mum's help, they carried it to their bedroom.

Ethan found a control panel and Louie got chairs and his favorite toy lion.

Louie had disappeared and run up the stairs and through the door holding sandwiches, snacks and drinks, he found a box and put the food into the rocket.

They climbed in and out of the rocket loading it with all sorts of things and soon it was ready.

"**WOW** Ethan" said Louie "our room is changing?"

Ethan looked up and screamed with excitement.

Standing in the same room as a giant rocket and the roof was missing.

They could see twinkling stars and the moon, "When did that happen?" they said, looking at each other.

There was a lot of hustle and bustle going on around them.

Ethan and Louie's bedroom had turned into a massive

rocket launch centre.

Ethan thought this was great, but Louie was more

worried about Mum coming up and seeing a rocket

and the roof missing from their room.

She would be really mad.

How would they explain this?

**A loud voice** boomed out, making them jump.

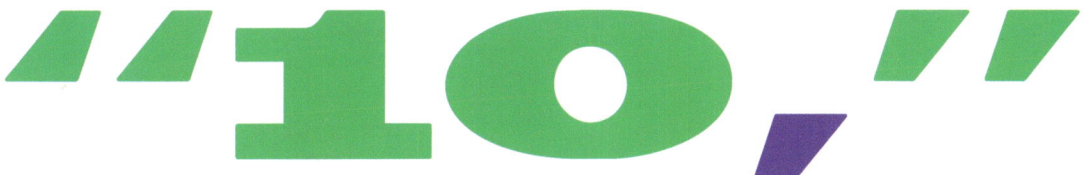

"What's going on?" Louie shouted.

"Why have you changed your clothes?" Ethan looked down and laughed.

"This is great…I'm an Astronaut…and so are you, Louie!"

**"No I am not!"** said Louie, until he saw his reflection.

**"Yes I am…!"**

**the loud voice** continued…

Ethan and Louie felt someone pushing them in the back.

"Let's move!" the voice said ", "You need to get in your rocket, NOW".

The **loud voice** continued...

Ethan was trembling with excitement.

"Really... are we going into space?" questioned Louie, turning a little **green**.

"It's so big" he whispered to Ethan, who was no longer listening to his brother.

**...the countdown went on.**

Ethan and Louie were pushed into their seats, strapped

in and their astronauts helmets pushed on.

The hatch slammed shut.

Dizzy with the excitement of being in their very own

rocket.

There were lots of flashing lights, buttons on the control

panel in front of them.

One of the buttons was flashing **Red** ... it said...

# "LAUNCH"

Again, the **loud voice** said...

Louie could not help himself and pressed the flashing

button, as the loud voice said blast off.

There was a very loud rumbling noise and the rocket started to shake.

Ethan and Louie looked at each other a little unsurely.

"Release the handbrake" **shouted the voice**.

Louie grabbed the handbrake and released it before Ethan had a chance to blink.

Without warning, the rocket blasts into the sky and shoots through the clouds.

Ethan screamed with delight.

**"Woohoo...!"**

Louie heard another rumbling noise.

"Oh no, I'm hungry" said Louie. "You will have to wait until we get to the Space Station", said Ethan, busy pressing buttons and flicking switches and steering the rocket. "The Space Station!" Louie said surprised. "Will that take long?".

"We are in space, Louie." "We can unbuckle our seat belts", commanded Ethan.

As Louie went to put his feet on the floor, he floated up out of his seat, he didn't like that.

Waving his arms about, Ethan laughed and laughed.

**"Stop it Louie, stop it."** Louie grabbed hold of a handle and refuses to let go. "Come on Louie," shouted his brother. "You need to just move your arms it's like swimming, watch me, and with that…Louie, let's go." They started floating around the rocket, in slow motion.

They were having fun floating around the rocket until…

**The voice ordered** "Prepare to dock at the Space Station".

Ethan pushed Louie toward the hatch.

He watched Louie float through the air...too funny, he thought.

He climbed into his seat and awaited orders from ground control.

At the hatch, Louie heard a loud bang, "What was that?" he called and held on tight.

Ethan said..."It's only the docking arm, Louie, when you see the astronaut through the window, open the hatch".

Louie saw the astronaut waving at him and waved

back, "Look, Ethan, he's waving at me!" shouted

Louie.

"Well, open the hatch," replied Ethan.

The astronaut spoke to Louie in Russian, but he couldn't understand him.

Ethan joined them, Ethan and shook the Russian's hand and said "Hello" in Russian.

"When did you learn Russian?" asked Louie.

"At school" said Ethan, laughing.

The next few minutes were spent floating between the rocket and the Space Station.

Louie wanted a closer look at the moon.

Ethan noticed Louie looking at the control panel.

"You must not touch anything on the space station!" Ethan said in a stern voice.

Louie was bored and found a computer screen.

He wondered if he could play his favorite video game.

He climbed into the astronaut's seat, but found he couldn't quite reach the controls.

He stretched out his arm as far as he could, but he still couldn't reach.

As he moved closer, to press the buttons, Ethan caught him.

**"STOP Louie"** shouted Ethan.  All the astronauts stopped and turned to look at Louie.

"I only just touched it, I didn't press any buttons" said Louie with a very **red** face, "I wanted to play my video game."

"Well, it's not on there", said Ethan, in a firm voice.

Soon it was time to get back into their rocket and set course for the moon.

Louie was excited, as he wanted to see if the moon was made of cheese.

They fastened the hatch and strapped themselves back into their seats.

Before long, they received the voice command, to separate the rocket from the Space Station.

Ethan pressed the Fire button to launch them toward the moon.

"Do you think the moon is made of cheese, Ethan?" asked Louie. "I don't know. Did you bring any crackers, just in case?" asked Ethan. Louie held up a big box of crackers...Ethan smiled...

Louie and Ethan stared out of the window, and saw the moon getting bigger.

Louie thought he saw moon people waving at him.

Ethan flew the rocket and landed on the moon and

inside a big crater.

Louie helped his brother carry out the equipment for

Ethan's science experiments.  "Now…" said Ethan,

"…while I'm doing my work, don't get into trouble."

Louie went off in search of Moon cheese, soon finding

a good amount, which he loaded into the rocket.

Before long, he had filled the rocket full of cheese.

Louie noticed Ethan talking to the moon people.

They looked angry, waving their arms around.

Just then, Ethan jumped and floated towards Louie.

Ethan whispered "What have you been doing?

The moon people have been watching you and said

that you have taken their cheese."

Inside the rocket, Ethan could not believe his eyes.

"**What did I tell you**…? Stay out of trouble.

You need to put some of their cheese back, it's not

ours and the rocket won't take off."  Ethan said "find

my seat, we need to get out of here now."

Ethan used his jetpack to get back to the angry moon people and his experiments, telling them that his brother was returning the cheese.

He quickly packed away his experiments and loaded them back into the rocket.

"Quick Louie, let's get out of here…if they see how much cheese we still have…" Ethan said.

He gave Louie an extra big push and he jumped back into the rocket, locking the hatch as quickly as he could.

The moon people, still angry, started banging on the hatch.

"Ethan, hurry" shouted Louie. Ethan flicked switches and pressed the **LAUNCH** button, **"Hold on tight**, Louie, this is going to be a bumpy take-off."

The rocket launched into Space, but the BANGING, on the hatch, was getting **LOUDER** and **LOUDER**. "Do you think the moon people are holding on?" Louie asked.

When the hatch burst open and together they both screamed......."**ARGHHHHH**...Mum! How did you get here?", "I live here" answered Mum.

Ethan and Louie looked at each other and then around their room.

What had happened? Who had fixed the roof?

Where was their rocket and cheese?

"Mum, I'm hungry" Louie said.

"That's good, because your dinner is on the table",

smiled Mum.

Both boys raced to the kitchen and tucked into fresh

and tasty cheese on toast.

They told mum all about their amazing adventure on

the rocket and stopping at the Space Station.

Meeting the Russian astronaut's and visiting the moon.

Louie told Mum that the moon people chased them

because he had collected all their cheese.

After their cheese on toast they went back to their

bedroom and carried on playing in the rocket their

Gran had bought them.

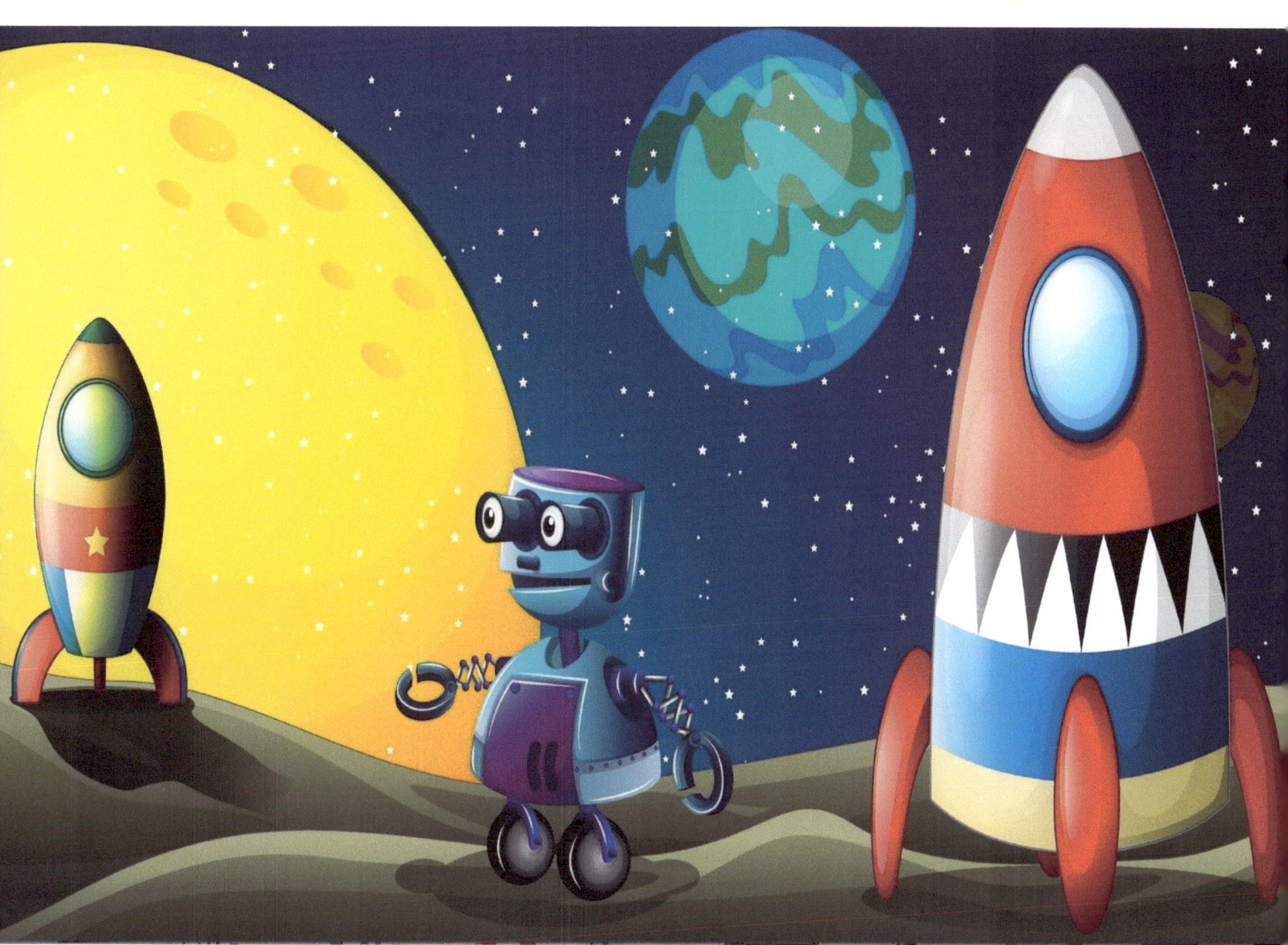

# More of Louie's adventures...

Dinosaurs in the Park

World Cup Louie

Louie lè Tour

Ethan the Elf

The Treasure Map

Detective Louie

www.ingramcontent.com/pod-product-compliance
Lightning Source LLC
Chambersburg PA
CBHW041011170626
46815CB00003B/260